Spot's Birthday Party

Eric Hill

It's Spot's birthday!

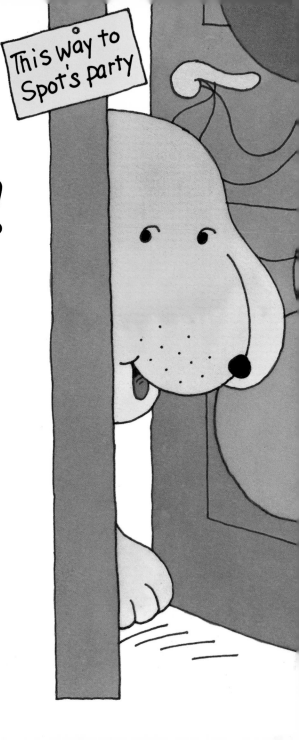

This way to Spot's party

Ready or not – here comes Spot!

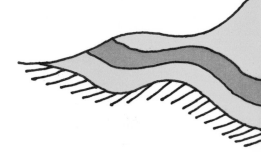

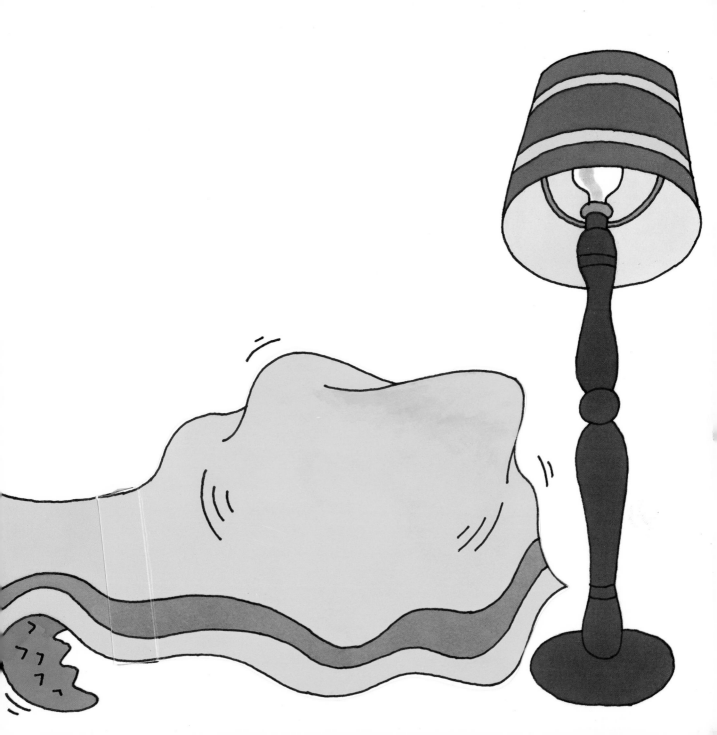

Spot has found someone behind the curtain ...

... and someone in the cupboard.

Come out, Spot can see you!

Somebody giggled. Look under the coat!

That's a silly way to hide!

Spot knows who's behind the door.

Who's that under the table?

Calm down, Spot!

PUFFIN BOOKS

Published by the Penguin Group: London, New York,
Australia, Canada, India, New Zealand and South Africa
Penguin Books Ltd, Registered Offices:
80 Strand, London WC2R 0RL, England
Penguin Putnam Books for Young Readers
345 Hudson Street, New York, NY 10014

Published in the United States of America by G. P. Putnam's Sons, 1982
Published in the UK by William Heinemann Ltd, 1983
Published in Puffin Books, 1985
First US paperback published by Puffin Books, 1999
Reissued 2003
3 5 7 9 10 8 6 4

Printed and bound in Malaysia

ISBN–13: 978–0–14250–125–2

ISBN–10: 0–14250–125–5